JAWBONE

MEGHAN
GREELEY

/J/A/W/B/O/N/E/

radiant press

Editor: Paul Carlucci
Cover art: Art Cohr
Book and cover design: Tania Wolk, Third Wolf Studio
Printed and bound in Canada at Friesens, Altona, MB

The publisher gratefully acknowledges the support of Creative Saskatchewan,
the Canada Council for the Arts and SK Arts.

Library and Archives Canada Cataloguing in Publication

Title: Jawbone / Meghan Greeley.
Names: Greeley, Meghan, author.
Identifiers: Canadiana 20230509339 | ISBN 9781998926008 (softcover)
Classification: LCC PS8613.R4255 J39 2023 | DDC C813/.6—dc23

radiant press

Box 33128 Cathedral PO
Regina, SK S4T 7X2
info@radiantpress.ca
www.radiantpress.ca

For Mallory,
when we shared a universe.

1.

The vocal cords do not atrophy. The larynx is a multi-purpose room. Of course, I swallow still. I clear my throat: a habit now, an empty signal.

The vocal cords look like a vagina. I have seen a video of this. They are fleshy pink bands slapping together. I once read about a man in the Ozarks who woke from a nineteen-year coma. He couldn't remember anything after 1984, the year of his accident, but seven thousand days of dormancy can't stop the cords from thrumming to life. He said *mama*. Then he said *Pepsi* and then he said *milk*. The brain goes soft, but the voice is always ready, waiting.

2.

If you think this video is *for* you, it's not. No—it's *for* you, but not *to* you. I'd explain it properly if you were here, but you're not here, and anyway, my mouth is wired shut. Well—the wires are gone now, but I'm still shut. I can't talk yet, but it isn't a head thing.

It is a head thing, you would probably say, or is your mouth on your ass?

I should say: it isn't a brain thing. I was wired shut, and then a man put his latex fingers in my mouth and cut out the wires with gardening shears, and now the ghosts of the wires wire me shut. Like when a fence is knocked down but you're in the habit of walking around it. You just walk right around it.

3.

This room is the world now. Here are the given circumstances: the world beyond these walls no longer exists, and so this one-room cabin has become my lone little planet. When a gale batters the tin roof, it is not a north wind but the solar winds or some such science thing, rattling me in my solitary orbit. I should clarify: the sun is still the sun in this scenario, but I have censored it like the proper nouns of a wartime letter. Heavy blackout curtains hang like never-evers, like the enemy must not discover light. Do these curtains hide a magic hour or a witching hour? I don't know, and the enemy wouldn't either. I bought them at a convenience store on the highway, the kind that sells cigarettes and canned soup but also party supplies and plastic barrels, and the plastic barrels were cash only. (Nothing else was cash only.) When I opened the package, a little nest of dead baby spiders tumbled onto the floor. They were mummified and milky, yet almost transparent in places. You know opals? Like that.

4.

Sometimes, when I sit in the dark, I try to listen to the Foley of the world. This whimper of metal is a swivel chair. That sigh of mass displacing air is me with my toes tucked under the seat, letting velocity twist me slowly, slowly clockwise, the pathway of time and unusual planets. I hear things you can't hear beneath a midday sun. I hear things you *can* hear beneath a midday sun too, but I hear them more so. Breathing. The acidic murmurs of my stomach. The beep of my watch: four in the morning. Astronauts still wear watches, like me.

I can hear the ocean. I try not to hear the ocean; I should acclimatize myself to the sounds of an ocean-less world. I should only perceive, as an exercise, the contents of this room: the creak of the iron cot, the wind in the cold woodstove. The groan of the floor, its boards settling with the night. Groaning under the weight of my suitcase, which vomits its contents onto the shiplap, because in my secret life I am messy, and besides, the camera can't see it.

I do not hear the camera, sitting silent and sentinel on its tripod, but I see it. I see its little light. I see it like a distant star whose radiation has found me here. It's the only thing that interrupts the darkness. A pinprick of red: recording.

The camera has been recording for thirteen minutes. The rules say that I am only allowed to speak for one minute. This was not the winning take. This was the seventy-eighth not-winning take. I knew it was another failed experiment the moment I pressed record and started listening to the light bulb. My head was beside a lamp, and I could hear electricity coursing through the filament. The bulb hummed in a key I didn't like, so I turned out the lamp and let the camera document the dark and the nothing and me in the dark with nothing to say.

5.

I found this cabin on Airbnb. I messaged the owner and said, I'm looking for the loneliest place in the world. I said, I'm in the market for an indefinite sojourn. I said, I'm looking for the kind of place that will make me feel like I'm the sole occupant of a distant planet without water or oxygen or microbial life. The owner messaged me back and said, I've never rented it for more than three nights but okay.

6.

I shower daily. I have been here for twenty-nine days and so I have taken twenty-nine showers and I have learned that this is the lifespan of a bar of Irish Spring soap if you are rigorous, which I am. I like the stench of it, of using this daily ritual as a marker of time. It takes three and a half hours for my dripping hair to dry completely. Once it is bone dry, the morning is over.

After the shower, my body is vermillion. The only way I feel clean is to scald my skin until it is red and raw.

This morning I walk barefoot and naked from the steaming bathroom to the blender. I make a smoothie from a banana and Greek yogurt and pomegranate juice and a stale cherry muffin. The smoothie is red, like me. Red as the light on the camera: still recording. I did not turn it off before falling asleep, I realize, and the memory card is robust.

I look at the camera and imagine I am on a YouTube cooking show. Just throw the whole muffin right on in there! That's what I'd say. That's the extent of my skill level. A few weeks ago, I'd continue, I put a slice of pizza in the blender with a dipping sauce. I had to add water because the pizza and the sauce would not liquefy.

Subscribers, I'd say with great solemnity, I don't recommend it.

I imagine that the YouTube video is removed because I am naked and it violates the terms of service. My nipples and the dark patch of hair between my legs have violated someone else's terms.

Maybe, I think, I will not say a minute's worth of words. Maybe I will show a minute of myself, exposed and unafraid, to prove that I have graduated beyond social conventions like shame of a naked body. Where I'm going, the rules won't apply.

I drink my muffin smoothie through a straw, sucking the thick, starchy liquid through my teeth. It's amazing how much living you can do without opening your mouth at all.

7.

I am not ashamed or afraid, but I am cold, so I dig through my suitcase with my toe. At the bottom of the pile is a wrinkled dress, red as the cherry stains on my fingers. I watch the camera watch me. Dangling from the tripod is a long strand of hair, my own, catching in the lamplight. Humans, I have read, shed nine thousand skins in a lifetime. My skin and my hair and my dust have left a trail across this room, across the lives of others and across this continent. It's hard to disappear, but I have plans.

8.

I would like to say that red is my favourite colour. I think that is convenient. Of all the questions they could ask us in the initial screening process, our favourite colour is the most important litmus test. But they don't ask us that. It sounds trivial, but it isn't. Haven't they thought this through? Because I have. I have thought about this extensively.

Things that we say are red but are not truly red:

Tomato soup (orange)
Raspberries (pink)
Red onion (purple)
Dried blood (black)

Things that are truly red:

Tomatoes
The Northern Cardinal
Celosia flowers
Your hair

The colour of your hair initially hovered between both lists. It might be auburn. If I could see it again, I would decide one way or the other. In my mind, it belongs on the second list and is the shade of red to which all other reds should be held accountable.

9.

I do not hear the coyotes. I do not hear the coyotes, which I know to be a crossbreed of coyotes and wolves, a brand-new beast that has disturbed the locals. I do not hear those mournful howls, a call and response from the treeline, an invitation to be found.

Unlike the beasts, I do not wish to be found. For a moment, I consider the reality that I will never be found, that you and I will now move through the years as strangers. The beasts howl, perhaps at each other, perhaps at the moon.

A boy once told me that girls love the moon. I shared this memory with you one night in the park. You snorted. You hated these gendered assessments, this offhand way, you exclaimed, of cramming every girl under the same parachute.

Do you mean umbrella, I said.

No, you said. Those suffocating circus things with handles, in school gymnasiums. You know the kind. That's where the girls are grouped.

I do know the kind, I said. When I was six I tore my labia on my own sneaker trying to crouch beneath one, balancing on my haunches, and thought I was bleeding out. That my insides were damaged.

You became emotional over this. Oh, my dearest dear.

It's a funny story, I insisted. But your eyes were misting over.

I just carry so much love for that little version of you in my heart, you said, laughing at yourself. I just want to hold her.

For a moment we were silent, gazing up at the night sky. You had never used the word love before, and you had never held me.

Above us the Buck Moon of July illuminated the world, bright as day. We lay on our backs in this silvery bath of wonder.

Shit, you sighed. Girls do love the fucking moon, don't they.

We decided that we could not argue with this boy's logic; I loved the moon, and you loved the moon, and the girls we knew, they also loved the moon. Every night, I said, we girls must marvel at that pale spectral as if seeing it for the first time. Sarah Kane says that theatre has no memory, I said, really onto something here. In the same way, girls have no memory of the night sky. Each time we fall in love with the moon all over again, night after night—

Until we die our girl deaths, you said.

Here in the cabin I have censored the moon as well as the sun. I will not fall in love with the moon again.

The beasts howl and howl. I do not think they sound hungry. I do not think this because I do not hear them. I should not hear them. I must detach myself from all terrestrial sounds or else this isn't a proper simulation.

10.

Wadi Rum is a true red in certain lights. It is a red gash in the earth, in the sandstone and the granite, like a wound. The valley is red because of the iron oxide. In Arabic, they call that place the Valley of the Moon and have called it that since before the Byzantine Era. Before we knew planets, before we had a Hubble or the Voyagers, the Jordanians guessed that our neighbours in the sky must be harsh and inhospitable. They assumed that what they could see with the naked eye, that silver spectral, could not possibly host life. And so they looked down and anointed the desert.

Now we know more about things we can't see so well with the naked eye, those planets no bigger than a freckle on a face. And now we know that Wadi Rum looks not like the moon but like Mars. It has served as a stand-in for Mars in so many films that it has probably manipulated the collective conscience as to what Mars truly looks like.

I have taped pictures of Wadi Rum to the ceiling here, so that the first thing I see when I wake is dust. I told Anatole about this strategy before I left. I was standing by a printer in a twenty-four-hour printing shop, and it was spitting out pixelated JPEGS of the desert. He said, You're taking this too far. Do you hear me? Are there wires clamping your ears shut too?

There was a Sharpie tethered to a string tethered to a table, so I wrote on a sheet of blank paper:

yes I am taking this far
225,000,000 million kilometres far

That paper costs six cents a page, said a man wearing a pocket protector.

11.

Tasks that take roughly one minute to perform:

Microwaving a small portion of leftovers
Finding the correct key on a keychain of many identical keys
Trimming the stems of one dozen roses
Walking down seven flights of stairs

You concocted this list. We were draped over the air conditioner, remember, wrapping ice cubes in cheese cloth and sucking them dry.

We barely knew each other when that first heat wave hit. I hadn't unpacked all my boxes yet, but the heat was our common enemy. It was one of the things that made us fast friends. The days were so hot that we kept wine in the freezer and ate it with spoons. We were dizzy with dehydration, so we drank.

We were listening to the radio. We did that together: listen to the radio. They were explaining the rules for the application process. Everybody was talking about it in those days. It was the only thing that anybody was talking about. Nobody could wrap their brains around the science-nonfiction.

A one-minute audition! I said. How to summarize the self in a minute? That isn't even time for the crazies to reveal themselves, for the judges to weed them out.

Are we still allowed to use that word? Crazy? you said, rolling ice cubes in your hand like dice. But I mean ... yes, every single person who applies will be a little bit crazy. They'd have to be.

Was the first cosmonaut crazy, I said, when he launched into space?

Yuri Gagarin, you retorted, believed he was coming back. Mars, you said, is a one-way trip. A journey to Mars is forever.

12.

It took us only a few minutes to decide, during our first conversation, that we should live together. We started late because you were late. When you finally blew into the rehearsal space, you apologized. You were late because a homeless man had spat in your face. There were still remnants of it, a long brown streak down your cheekbone. He was chewing tobacco, you said. You were startled because the pedestrians around you pretended not to see. You stood there, frozen, music still coursing through your headphones while the man wiped his mouth on the back of his hand and retreated under his blue tarp.

You weren't mad at the homeless man, you said. You had heard strange mutterings from under the tarp. You thought he was mentally very far away. You didn't say mentally ill. You said *very far away*. Like he wasn't sick—he was just travelling. You were mostly angry, you said, at the passersby, too anesthetized to react.

We waited until you came back from the washroom, your face scrubbed clean and raw. The colour had risen in your cheeks from the friction of the harsh paper towel, the pink industrial hand soap. You apologized again, but the room was on your side. Suddenly there were sides. If a homeless man spat on me, said the director, I would've turned around and walked home again and sterilized my skin in boiling water and bleach.

If *I* saw a homeless man spit on a young woman, said an actor, I'd like...And he clicked his tongue on the roof of his mouth. Like the plop of a leaky tap. You flinched and said nothing.

You sat in the folding chair beside me. When the director paused to check an email, you leaned toward me, asked me for hand lotion. Your face was stinging from the soap. I said it was scented, was that ok, musk, maybe strong for the face. But you accepted the little tube and massaged your cheek. Ah, you said, now I smell like a man.

You opened your sketchbook. I'm the costume designer, you said. You've got shoulders like a velvet hanger, you said. You said: Where did you and your shoulders come from?

But you didn't ask me. You asked the me that you were sketching on the page, the costume you were hanging there.

I said: I'm new. I said: I'm subletting a basement up north.

You nodded, cocking your head with each pencil stroke. You were very focused on my clavicle. I heard there were over a hundred applicants for your role, you said. You must be dynamite.

I lowered my voice. I think I was hired because I was the only person who auditioned who could play the concertina. Apparently that's an important part of the script?

You grinned. Your pencil hovered over the silhouette of my throat, the lines more slender than reality. You said: Did you move here alone?

I said: My boyfriend moved to California to study civil engineering or maybe chemical engineering, I'm not sure which, and now it's too late to ask. I'm in too deep. I said: He moved there and I moved here and now he writes me emails and it's very romantic.

You said: Why didn't you move to California?

I said: I didn't want to live in a perfect climate because then what would I yearn for?

You looked up from the page me to the real me. Oh, Velvet, you said, have I got a room for you.

13.

Mine would be the bigger room. Your previous roommate, you said, had been a medical student, had been selected for a residency somewhere out west. I stood in the doorway, taking in the room's high ceilings, the healthy philodendron she'd left behind, perfectly centred on a curtain rod in one of the tall windows. I didn't know it was called that yet, philodendron, but you knew plants and how to take care of them. In the living room, a jade pothos you'd had for years spilled all the way to the floor. You did not abandon things.

I thought of the tiny brown mushrooms growing under the baseboard heaters in my current apartment. I thought, perhaps I can cultivate a greener sort of garden.

The landlord is an ass, you said, but I like buildings that existed before Technicolour.

I looked at the wide crown mouldings and their ornate millwork at the corners, the cracks in the plaster. What year was it built? I said.

The landlord said it was pre-war.

Which war?

Hmm?

Why do we say pre-war, as though the wars ever stopped?

You grinned at me from the threshold. Velvet, you said, please move in with me.

In a city of strangers, it felt nice to be your chosen one.

This is your home, I said, you should at least take the bigger room—it has more windows, more light.

It'll be your home now, you said. And then you raised your arm, showed me the cosmos of freckles there. Besides, I'm a redhead, you said. I've gotta keep these babies in the dark.

14.

Baby—

I'm so glad to hear that you've found an apartment with a nice girl. I think it would be very good for you to make a female friend. I've noticed that you don't really have any. Sometimes girls feel that they "just get along better with men," but this is problematic—misogynist, even—as they are essentially trying to be "one of the guys" and are distancing themselves from the tenets of their gender. Women do not have to make themselves men to advance in society. Women can just be women. And I think it would be wonderful for you to have a girl to do things with and talk to about work and life and boys (ha ha).

Love,
D

15.

That first night, I ate my dinner alone, washed my dish, and returned it to its cupboard. Half an hour later, you ate your dinner alone, washed your dish, and returned it to its cupboard. You knocked on my door and said: I'm thinking of making gulab jamun for dessert, but only if you help me eat it. You had learned how to make it in Nepal. I have this good recipe, you said, but maybe you know a better one?

I hadn't been to Nepal and didn't know what gulab jamun was, so I said I wasn't hungry. I said I wasn't hungry so I didn't have to say that I wasn't cultured or interesting or well-travelled.

You closed the door and I read a little bit about Nepal.

You didn't make gulab jamun that night. We listened to different music in different rooms with the volume low. When we passed in the hallway as I unpacked, we apologized for nothing and walked around each other. Wherever I stepped, the floors creaked; you, an old cartographer of the more problematic floorboards, floated in assured silence. I smiled at you once as I passed like we were two guests at the same hotel.

It's hard, someone once told me, to make new friends once you're an adult.

I knocked on your wide-open door and asked would you mind if I took a bath. You said that I didn't need to ask.

I just wanted to make sure you didn't have to pee, I said. The words sounded juvenile coming from my mouth.

I could always pee on the ficus, you said.

Right, I said.

The freckles on your nose scrunched together. I'm kidding, Velvet.

Ha!

You're shy for an actor.

But I'm not quiet once you get to know me, I said.

When I returned to my room afterward, wrapped in a bathrobe, the closet door was shut. I stopped because I hadn't shut the door. I definitely hadn't shut the door before, or had I?

Then the closet was a living thing. From inside came muffled giggles, and I stood there, hair dripping. I stood there not knowing whether to open the door and say something like: Jig's up! But then you giggled louder, and I knew you knew I could hear you and that this was always the point: an offering. You were trying to blast your way through the bow shock of the universe, where the interstellar winds mean no more boundaries. I began to giggle because we were both in on it—the joke was ours. It was ours.

You tumbled out of the closet, and then I wasn't quiet anymore.

16.

Hi baby,

Thanks for your email! I'm enjoying this new epistolary phase of our relationship. Very Dickensian, don't you think? Ha ha ha.

The play sounds interesting!... Though I admit that the concept may be over my head. I am, after all, a mere plebian. While I know what the words your director used to describe his concept mean individually—Chekhov, live music, technocratic dystopia, ecopoetics, Anthropocene, maximalism, borscht—I admit that I can't quite picture how they all work together to form a cohesive play. But that is why you are the artist, not me!

You know what I was thinking about today? That time we drove up the coast to see the drift ice. I'd never seen ice like that before. Nothing like that in the Old Country, ha ha. I'm attaching a photo I took of you that day, in your red coat. I miss that smile.

Love you always,
D

17.

You sewed buttons on a costume. There were dollar-store reading glasses on your nose. You looked old and wise. You said you hated to work with your hands when your brain wasn't stimulated. I suggested Netflix, audiobooks. John Slattery, I said. He does audiobooks. *A Farewell to Arms.*

You said: *Fuck* Hemingway. You said: If I never read another Hemingway novel in my life, it'll be one too many. You said: Read to me while I sew, I like your voice better than John Slattery's. You told me there was wine in the fridge, a big juice box of it. You said: Let's get drunk and get literary.

I plucked a book from the shelf and said: I found this book inside a barbecue. I found it inside a barbecue, I said, at a dead man's estate sale.

It felt like a good story. I felt like the story made my life sound a certain kind of way, like it featured certain kinds of characters. When my old drama professor died, I said, telling the story, paramedics struggled to open the door. There were books stacked floor to ceiling, four rows deep. There were books in the kitchen cupboards, books in the bathtub.

Get out, you said.

No one knows how he washed. He owned two cars, one in his garage and one in his driveway. The one in his driveway was the one he drove. He kept crisp white driving gloves in the glove compartment. Imagine: a glove compartment used for gloves. The second car was an empty shell. He'd removed the engine, gutted the interior of its seats, and filled it with books. When he died, they opened the doors of the house and the garage and let us glean new literature from a hoarder and his habits. I found a book in the backyard, over old charcoal, like dinner was waiting. *Sex at Dawn: How We Mate, Why We Stray, and What It Means for Modern Relationships.*

I stopped the story. I didn't say that I had accidentally imagined the book in his hands. I didn't say that I had accidentally pictured him reading it in bed, maybe one hand on the book and one hand somewhere else. I didn't say that this made me feel queasy, probably because he was dead. I just said: The brain aneurysm killed him in less than a minute.

Later, when you were concocting your list of things a person can do in a minute or less, you remembered this story. It takes one minute or less to die.

18.

Our home smelled of Baltic amber. Those were the candles you'd buy, thick pillars from the bookstore. Amber itself smells like nothing, not even the life it traps. Perfumers play with our synesthesia. They name a scent for amber because the fragrance makes us feel the way amber looks. A warm glow, a certain slant of light. An illusion made with labdanum resin, benzoin, balsam of Peru, frankincense, myrrh, copal, sometimes cedarwood, sometimes sandalwood, sometimes vanilla. (You hate vanilla.) The modern word comes from *ambergris:* excretion from a sperm whale, a fatty material straight from the intestine. Salt water and sun massage the stink from it until it is earthy. Sweet. Ambergris is almost impossible to find.

When you opened the door to your room, I smelled the resin flowing. It was confusing because I saw you drying your hair, but I smelled the ancients and their ceremonial pyres. It was weird because I saw you watering your yucca cane, but I smelled the magma of the Earth. It was disorienting because I saw you reading, but I smelled dusk falling over a deep canyon. I saw you seeing me, and I said: I smell firelight, ha ha.

19.

Baby—

I'm glad to hear that the show is going well. Have you given further thought to moving here while I finish my program? To be honest, I don't understand why an actor would prefer to move anywhere other than Los Angeles. Isn't this a mecca for "actor types"?

Last night I went to a party for the graduate students. It was organized by the faculty and it was truly wonderful, baby. They served amuse-bouches as a starter. It was so refreshing to eat an appetizer that actually fits in the mouth and can be consumed properly in one bite—not like all these gigantic American appetizers you see. The people of this continent are rather obsessed with size and quantity.

Last night reminded me of the summer I went to the Black Sea, when I was a child. We ate amuse-bouches in a restaurant that had lamps on the tables. Someday I want to take you there, baby. You'd like it.

Love you baby,
D

20.

The director had a new vision, and that vision was water. We would stand in water. Water would fall from the ceiling from rain wands. Water, he said, would represent the fluidity of time.

I raised my hand. The concertina can't get wet, I said.

What's that?

The concertina. It can't get wet.

No?

The bellows are made of cardboard.

He scratched his chin, his enthusiasm deflating a little. Huh, he said. I felt like one of those Difficult Actors.

You were present at this rehearsal, sitting off to one side. I could see you looking despairingly at the delicate fabric samples in your lap.

And then he said your name. You looked up, but the director was still looking at me.

I mean, how *much* moisture is too much moisture? he said. He seemed very taken aback that not all instruments are waterproof. He called me by your name again.

Everyone was confused. Anatole, another actor in the cast, corrected him.

The director blinked, shook his head. Sorry, sorry!

I wondered how he had made this mistake, when we look nothing alike, when our names sound nothing alike. I felt a strange pride that in his head we were all tangled up together, you and I. Synonymous. We locked eyes across the room.

So, question, said Anatole. Will the water be *cold?*

The director nodded reluctantly. I don't know how we'd keep it warm, he said. But in the world of the play, it *would* be cold. So at least you won't have to *act* like it's cold because it actually *will* be.

There was a general murmur around the room. Right, said Anatole, very slowly, dragging out the vowel.

I raised my hand. I too am made of cardboard, I said.

I hadn't meant to be funny, but no one laughed harder than you.

21.

You sharpened an eyebrow pencil and gave me a beauty mark beside my left eye, like Sherilyn Fenn. You brought me to a party in an apartment over a used electronics shop, the home of a playwright you had vowed to fuck before the leaves turned. The Belvedere Torso, we called him. Not because of his stomach—just because of the way he leaned to scribble notes with his right hand. It looked uncomfortable.

The light bulbs were red and the air smelled like sage and sweat. I didn't know anyone, so you promised not to leave my side, but somehow I lost you between the bathroom line and grabbing more beer from the case on the balcony.

I hugged my bottle and looked for you. As long as I was moving, I had purpose. As long as I was actively searching, I wasn't the person standing alone, staring into the middle place.

I walked into the kitchen and heard someone say: When is an apple dead?

When you pick it, said a girl who was sitting on the counter, her legs crossed twice over in a way that made her look like an Olympian or a pretzel.

An apple isn't dead when you pick it, said a man. I couldn't tell which man was speaking. Apples bruise *after* they've been plucked from the stem, he continued. You can't bruise a dead thing.

So what, then? When it rots? The pretzel girl had discovered the speaker and was studying him.

The man said: Sure.

I dunno, said the pretzel girl. Humans decay because they're dead. Rotting doesn't mark the moment of death.

The man said: You're thinking about this in a very egocentric way.

How's that?

You're thinking about this like a human. We die differently.

How's that?

The cortex, he said.

The man was wearing a toque, too hot for this weather. A toque rolled tightly at the brim until it was tiny—so tiny that it might continue to roll up like a condom and fly from his scalp.

But then at what point in the rotting is the apple dead, demanded a new voice—yours. It carried over the music, over the voices and the bottles against bottles and thumps on plaster and flames eating wooden wicks. You're either alive or you're dead, you said. There's no iffiness in death. Rotting is too slow a burn.

You stood in the doorway and held your beer and waited for an answer.

He thought for a moment, searching for something to say. He clearly had not thought about this before speaking. He clearly had not thought about this at all. When it decays and the seeds leave it, he said finally.

So when it achieves its reproductive functions, it's done? It's free to die then?

No, I—

Sounds like you're thinking about it like a man, you said.

Everyone looked from you to the condom hat man to you to the condom hat man. Someone whistled.

Maybe, said the man in a hopeful voice, an apple is only dead once it's been eaten.

Later, we laughed about this on our couch while we drank gin and put bras on our heads and pretended we were dumb men.

22.

Baby–

I used to think that maraschino cherries and almonds taste the same to certain people. Like how some people are weird about cilantro because they think it tastes like soap. But then I found out that ever since the war, maraschino cherries have been preserved in sugar syrup and the oil of bitter almonds. Did you know that in order to achieve that bright red colour, they are soaked for three weeks in a dye? The dye is called Red #40. I recently read a study indicating that Red #40 contains benzidine and 4-aminobiphenyl, which have been known to cause cancer and allergies in children. Do you eat many maraschino cherries, baby? It would probably be best to avoid sweets containing them or alcoholic beverages in which they are used. It is probably best to avoid red cocktails altogether, just to be safe.

Have you been drinking much? I recently bought a water bottle that glows when it's time to drink water. Now I drink whenever the light tells me to and it's wonderful to not have to remember something so banal as hydration when I have been in the library for fourteen hours reading Vitruvius. I have been drinking so much water every day and I think it's making me smarter, baby. Are you drinking enough water?

Love you,
D

23.

Will it hurt, I said, and you said: Oh yeah. You said: Name your damage.

I said: I want what you have, what do you have?

You wouldn't show me yet. You stuck a needle into the pink eraser of an HB pencil and asked me for the alcohol, and I said, It's over the fridge, you know that, but you said, No, the rubbing alcohol, the kind you *don't* drink.

But we didn't have any. So you got the drinking kind and said: Actually, this will help.

You poured vodka into tumblers and remembered that you had antibacterial hand sanitizer, but it wasn't regular, it was pine. You said: I hope you don't mind smelling like the forest.

I said: What if you fuck it up.

Take off your shirt, you said, and think about something else.

You came toward me with the needle, a bead of ink glistening at the tip. Certain things make me dizzy, I said. Things where they don't belong. Like staples in a napkin or those Christmas decorations people make, cloves pushed into the rinds of oranges to make patterns.

Like a penis in a vagina, you said, and we laughed.

You tried to distract me with something you had read, something about an artist named Derrick Santini. He had made a lenticular image that appeared to move as you walked around it. *A Fool for Love*, it was called. It had been on display a few years ago at a gallery in the UK. It showed a woman lying on her back and a swan between her thighs, raping her—Leda and the swan.

One day, you said, a police officer was riding a bus past the gallery and he saw the piece through the window. And he was absolutely horrified.

Rape is horrifying, I agreed.

Wait, you said. So he gets some other police officers and they go to the gallery, and they demand that the piece be taken down. But get this: they didn't want the photograph taken down because it depicted a scene of rape. You know why they wanted *A Fool for Love* taken down?

Why? I said, as the needle went deep.

Because it promoted bestiality, you said.

I said: There's a special place in hell for cops and swans.

You said: There ought to be a penal colony for people like that.

When you were done, I stood in front of a mirror and held up another mirror and angled it so I could see. The area below my shoulder was red and angry. There was a circle of dark ink, a perfect circle. You had steady hands from all that cutting and sewing. Inside the circle was another circle, a solid little circular dot.

It's a boob, I complained. You gave me a tit tattoo!

It isn't a *boob*, you said, and showed me yours.

You peeled off your shirt and you were not wearing a bra. I focused my eyes on the boob on your back. I focused my eyes very hard on the boob on your back.

It's not a boob, you said again. It's alchemy. It's the symbol for gold. The perfection of all matter.

You put your shirt back on and wiped my blood from the tip of the needle with some toilet paper.

Gold, you said, is the apex of spiritual, physical, and mental wealth.

It sounded like you were saying lines from a movie about a journey, and I told you this and you laughed until your ears popped—like you were on a plane, you said. Like you were scaling a mountain and reaching the summit.

We got drunk and I shouted that I have a boob on my back but it's okay because between me and my best friend we have two tits or possibly six depending on how you look at it and together we're a sexy woman! We are the queen of a distant planet! Bow!

24.

Baby–

How are things? Your last email was a little brief. You haven't mentioned your roommate much—are you girls getting along? Have you ever visited the website WikiHow? There is a wealth of information on this site, which can be useful for people who are grappling with simple problems but are perhaps too embarrassed to ask for advice or help. I found an article that I think might help you get to know your roommate better. The article is called HOW TO MAKE FEMALE FRIENDS. *There are many different steps that might seem a little asinine, but sometimes the best way to learn something is to forget everything you thought you knew about it and start from scratch. I know how shy you can be—maybe give this a shot. Let me know how it goes. But then again, if you aren't making friends, maybe it's a good indication of something greater. Maybe that city is just not the one for you. Have you thought any more about visiting once the play closes?*

Cheer up,
D

25.

In the evenings, we will eat profiteroles and drink wine from the Rhône Valley with our fingers wrapped around real crystal stems. We will walk barefoot over a thick pile rug, handwoven, pale white fibres threaded with blues, the colours of the Adriatic Sea. You will play the piano, nocturnes to make us drowsy. I will play the concertina with the windows open, because we will be living in a flat in Paris, and this is what happens in Paris. Music drifts from all the open windows. We will drink oolong tea from china cups and let them gather water rings on the night tables as we fall asleep in layers of gossamer satin.

This is the game we played when we were falling asleep. We texted each other from our separate beds, and we could hear each other giggling through the thin wall, but the joke was that we didn't speak. The joke was that when we die and we are famous and they publish a volume of our letters, those will be our letters. Those little blue texts will be the window to our brains and our souls and our lifelong friendship.

We'll be an HGTV *special,* you typed, *where people tell us the in-jokes they spin with their lovers, like living in a tree house, like hopping on a freighter and sailing the Northwest Passage, and then we'll do it to show that maybe lovers should do the things they dream of doing in the first six months before the dreams die.*

We'll need men to act as our lovers, I replied.

Ha ha, you said, *good nite queen!*

26.

When I think of you now, there are often pins in your mouth.

I did not like it when there were pins in your mouth. I was always afraid you would trip and the pins would puncture your tongue. But you were graceful. I had never seen you run to catch a bus. You moved through the world like steady water.

Your apprentice on the play was young and chatty. You were teaching her how to do a fitting, where to place all those pins for later reference. We were in a storage room, the three of us, and you were cinching me in black, shimmery fabric. Your hands never once touched my body. Like this, you said, mumbling through those dizzying pins.

When you had finished, you stepped out of the room, waiting for the garment. Your apprentice stayed to help me undress, to help me avoid jabbing myself on the frock full of porcupine dangers. Safely disrobed, I reached for my shirt.

You have *amazing* boots, said the apprentice.

The compliment felt strange. I looked down. They were not my boots. They were part of my costume, boots that she had laced me into ten minutes earlier, boots that she herself had chosen with your guidance.

Thank you, I said.

I've seen a lot, she continued cheerfully. And yours are just so damn perky!

She had already left the room by the time I realized I'd misheard her. I looked in the mirror and saw you in the doorway, frowning. You had overheard.

Everything okay? you said.

I said: Oh yes.

It wasn't okay for her to comment on your body like that, you said.

It's okay.

It's not okay Velvet. I'm sorry. I'll talk to her. You sighed and popped those pins back in your mouth, moving away.

I stared at my chest in the full-length mirror, the dim work light throwing strange shadows. I liked that you were protective of my body. But I wondered if you disagreed with her evaluation of it.

27.

From my window, through the philodendron, I watched as a man in overalls painted a sign above the new business across the street. I didn't know people still did that—painted signs. I watched his brush form letters in some antiquated font. I lit a candle. I felt plucked out of time.

Anatole did an acrobatic tumble into my room. He was crashing on our couch for a while between sublets. Where, he said, is my *phone?* This, admittedly, ruined the illusion and catapulted me to the present.

I carried my candle all over the house searching for the phone. He found it in his back pocket. I don't know how he hadn't felt it during the tumble.

By the time I glanced through the kitchen window, the sign was finished. THE FURNACE MAN, it read. I shivered, the candle flame shivering with me. We live across from a crematorium now, I said.

You peered up from the table where you were stripping thyme from its tiny twigs. You were always cooking. Good, you said. I won't have far to go in the end.

Do *not*, Anatole said, have me *cremated*.

Why? you said.

Because *ow*.

You wouldn't feel it.

I thought of your hair engulfed in flames. I didn't like it.

I need a headstone, said Anatole. I want the attention.

You rubbed your hands together. The kitchen was fragrant.
Underground seems like the loneliest place on Earth, you said.

Why? said Anatole. Everyone else is there.

Later, after he'd gone out to kiss some boys, and you were draping
fabric around the sewing mannequin you'd named Judy, you
spoke without looking at me.

If you outlive me, you said, would you scatter me somewhere?

Where?

I don't care. I just don't want to be in the urn alone.

We could share one, I said.

Yeah?

It would probably save us a lot of money.

And we are on a budget.

Our ashes can just mix for eternity.

I need to update my will, you said.

I said: I suppose I need a will.

You pushed pins into Judy's ribcage. I was lonely before you came, Velvet.

I had never thought of you as a person who might be lonely. But before I could answer, Anatole returned and did a cartwheel into the room. We're all *idiots*, he announced. The Furnace Man is a store that sells HVACs.

28.

The evening of our dress rehearsal, there was a bouquet of flowers on the table in the green room, an arrangement so big that actors sitting on opposite couches had to crane their necks around it. There were many flowers I didn't know the names of, curling, frothy shy things the colour of red wine, white puffy ones that looked like roses in need of antihistamines.

They're for you, Velvet, you said, brushing past me with a vest in your hands, sewing an errant button. You winked.

My stomach dropped. I hadn't gotten you anything. I should have gotten you something. I wondered if you'd gotten something for everyone or just me, because we were roommates, because we were synonymous, because we had become a unit. But why tonight? Why not tomorrow, for opening, as per custom?

Oh, I said, that's so nice. I didn't . . .

Oh, they're not from me, babe, you said.

You had never called me babe before. I looked at the tag.

Break a leg (not an accordion!)
– D

I guess he got the dates mixed up, I said.

I need a boyfriend, Anatole sulked, sprawling onto the couch and posing like a life drawing model. How did you meet? Does he have a brother? Or a hot dad?

He moved to my hometown when we were in high school, I said. He was smart and from a country I had never been to.

Cute accent? Anatole said. Cuter than mine?

It's a beautiful arrangement, you said. I love a *ranunculus*.

You fingered one of the white puffy ones with the same hand that held a threaded needle. In my head, you said it like an insult: ranunculus. It was a disappointing name for a beautiful flower. A hideous, common thing.

29.

Baby—

Did you get the flowers? Sorry about the card. NOT accordion!!
Concertina. I should know that by now.

Oops,
D

30.

On opening night, you did not bring the playwright you'd been
flirting with. Instead, I saw you kissing the lead act-res when
you disappeared outside for a cigarette together.

She called herself that: an actress. I called her an actor once,
and she corrected me: act-*ress*. Why would you want to erase
your cunt, she said.

Now the actress slid her hand under your dress, toward your
cunt. Your hair looked orange in the streetlight.

Anatole followed my gaze. That surprises exactly no one, he
said, clinking his glass to mine. Cheers for queers. Lord knows
we need numbers.

31.

It is hard to carry three drinks if you have small hands. The trick is: you don't. You just drink the third one. And then you drink one more so you aren't double fisting. I bought a drink for you and a drink for the actress to be nice, but I couldn't find either of you so I drank them one-two and then I had one left because math.

I said this to Anatole as I waved around the vodka soda that wasn't in my belly yet. I'm a single fister, I said. I like to keep the other hand free for emergencies.

He said: Do you want to sit down?

I said: Do you want this? If you take it, I'll have zero.

Anatole said: I'm a tequila girl.

I drank my drink and it went down the wrong way. My throat closed and I wanted to cough but I couldn't cough because my throat was clamped shut, so I choked. I tried to choke very quietly because beside me the director was talking to a critic about the oppressive weight of our endless parade of yesterdays.

Do you need a thump on the back? said Anatole. You're snotting *everywhere*.

I slipped away into the bathroom to choke in private. I locked myself in a stall and my throat felt tighter and I couldn't breathe and I would have thrown up if I were the kind of person who throws up. I heard footsteps, so I tried to choke more quietly, but there was water coming from my nose and my eyes and probably my ears and every other orifice.

Hey, said Anatole, knocking on the door. Will you survive, do you think?

I coughed until I had enough oxygen for one good cough that cleared the air. And he pushed open the door and pressed toilet paper to my face. Jesus, he said. You're like a cat. If you're choking, don't *retreat to die.*

I took the deep breath of life and asked the main question I wanted answering, the one that had been really bugging me. What the fuck, I said, is an amuse-bouche?

Girlfriend, he said, it's probably when your pussy is amused by the feeble attempts of a man to please it.

32.

I woke up with a tongue dry as cardstock and remembered the rain eddying down my jawline on the solitary walk home, down to where the choking tears had already made a home, rolled out a welcome mat.

I said nothing as I heard you go about your day, as last night's wine left your bloodstream, as you ate a bagel and the actress ate one of our bagels. As you both shared a whispered, giggling conversation as she waited for an Uber.

When I walked into the kitchen, I said nothing. I said nothing for such a long time that I was saying something.

You said: What's up?

I said: You could've told me.

You said: Told you what?

I said: Told me that I shouldn't wait for you at the bar, because I looked for you and I couldn't find you and I didn't know if you were okay.

Sorry, you said. I wasn't expecting—

You don't have to explain, I said and closed the cutlery drawer very, very quietly so that it didn't make a sound that sounded on purpose. If you didn't feel like this was a thing that you could share with me, I said, you don't have to feel guilty about it.

Jesus, what are you talking about? I tell you everything.

Not everything, though. Obviously.

I didn't like that I said the word obviously. It made the sound that a hand makes when it lands on a hip. I flushed. You flushed too.

Why are you mad at me right now? you said.

I'm not mad, I said, playing with a loose screw on the drawer handle.

You're acting pretty mad, you said.

It's just that I almost died, I said. It's just that I bought you and Whatshername drinks and I couldn't find you, so I drank them and I choked on them. Well, I didn't choke on those ones, I choked on mine, but anyway it's just as well because Whatshername doesn't drink soda water because she says it makes her burp. She burped a lot in rehearsals, and maybe she has an ulcer. I think I should tell her that she should get checked for an ulcer, or maybe you should tell her? Maybe it would be better coming from you?

Are you hungover or drunk still? you said.

I thought she was very good in the show, I said. I thought your costume looked very beautiful on her.

I wanted to open the cutlery drawer and climb inside it. But instead I just walked past you, past your parted lips. I shut the door to my bedroom and picked up my phone. *When is a good time for me to come to California?* I typed and pressed send.

33.

You watched me pack. The radio was playing.

They're talking about the Mars thing again, you said, and you reached for the volume.

When that first shuttle launches, said the radio, it'll be the biggest media event of all time!

The most famous people on Earth, said a co-host, are going to be the human beings millions of kilometres away from it!

You watched me roll my skirts into neat little balls. I roll my clothes when I pack too, you said. I've always thought it's the most efficient way to do it.

I said: Yeah.

You said: They're talking about Mars like it's some great honour. You can never lay eyes on your home again, or see your family again, or sleep in your bed again, or see a tree again, or buy a Happy Meal again, or swim again, or scratch a mosquito bite again, or go to the library again, or ride a bike again, or hold your lover again. That's death.

I said: Who should go, then?

You said: Only people who deserve it.

I said: Like who?

Your phone vibrated. It was the actress, calling you. I saw her name on the screen. I turned away and folded a dress. I didn't roll it. I folded it, and I laid it on top of everything.

Your phone vibrated and vibrated. Go ahead, I said, answer it. And can you turn off the radio on your way out? I have an early flight.

You turned off the radio and went into your room and the vibrating ended.

34.

He said: Welcome to the land of milk and honey.

We drove past a field of wind turbines, white and uniform as the gravestones of soldiers, oscillating forever on the scorched plains. My teeth felt different in California. The dry air rippled through the exposed nerves. The unfilled cavity in my left molar made itself known.

His teeth were different in California too. He was handsome in the north, like a bookish underwear model. He had always been too handsome for me; in school, the prettier girls of the upper echelons had reminded me how lucky I was. But here, his pale European complexion looked pallid in the bright Pacific light. The yellow sun made his teeth yellow at the roots, subtle, apparent maybe only to me, who spent so much time looking at his mouth.

His kiss tasted different in California too. It was stale, like the air released from an inflated balloon.

35.

Are you having fun? you texted. *Miss you.*

Then, later: *I feel like things are weird between us? Can we talk?*

When I didn't answer for several days, you texted that you were going to change your phone keyboard to the languages of other lands—the lands, you said, to which we would someday travel. You knew none of the words, so you slid in letters more beautiful than our own: *ОУ! Miss yoц so мцсж.*

A day later, I typed: *Gööð night, löve yöu, tælk söön.* I stared at it for one full minute before deleting it.

Then I typed: *in Cali everyone has a necklace with a pendant in the shape of their own name.*

And I flipped my pillow to the cool side, not waiting for your reply.

36.

The hot winds of the Santa Anas licked brush fires. They began to ration the water: no washing cars, no watering lawns. A beige film settled on everything, dulling the shine of cars on the turnpikes, even the expensive models. Dust was the great equalizer. Now you couldn't tell a Porsche from a Hyundai. The poverty and the opulence blending together, all beige and dull and dirty.

We ate cold fish and cold potatoes and salad chilled in the refrigerator, or we ate out. He sucked air through his teeth when I suggested a bucket of chicken. His teeth were dying at the roots, and I was worried about it. I was pretty worried.

Let's go for a drive, he said one night.

I was sitting on the floor, pretending to read Dostoevsky. He had said to me once: You should read Dostoevsky. You should read Conrad, Zola.

Now he said: Never mind Dostoevsky, it's hot. He stood over me, tall and skinny and perspiring. He said: Aren't you hot?

There are three things that I like about myself: my eyebrows, my handwriting, and the fact that I don't sweat. I said: No, it's not so bad.

Come, he said.

We drove fast and listened to music so loud that we didn't have to speak. He pulled into a parking lot shaded by a grove of lemon trees, near a baseball diamond. The bleachers were dark, deserted. Lights from passing cars flickered in snatches through the foliage. He cranked his seat back as far as it would go. He said: Do you want to live here, you and me, under the bleachers? Forever?

I dunno, I said. I feel like we should at least live close to a convenience store.

He said: I'm proud of you for reading the Dostoevsky. Do you like it?

I said: I don't comment on a book until I've finished it. It's important to know the end before I judge the beginning.

He kissed me. I closed my eyes and wanted something that wasn't quite this but was maybe coming. I looked past him to the shadowy diamond. The grass was dewy. I wondered if they were allowed to water baseball diamonds, whether the rules for sprinklers applied when it came to fun and games. His real belt and his seat belt clanged together like a cowbell, and he did away with both and mine too. I said: How nice, the grass is wet.

37.

In the here and now of the cabin, a sudden flutter of movement in the corner of my eye makes me jerk my foot to the floor, stopping my slow oscillation. I have fallen asleep in the chair, and the camera is once again documenting my silence. I rub my eyes. I can do this now; it's been fifty-three days since I last wore mascara. The last time I wore mascara, I was speaking.

Whenever I rub my eyes now, I luxuriate in the action. Many women never get to touch their eyelids. When I was young, an older boy told me that if I wanted to know what a penis felt like, I should rub my eyelid. I wasn't old enough for makeup then, so I tried it out, wondering if it was true. It was, I think.

I rub my eyes and I blink. The flutter, again. It comes from near the camera and then settles there, a thing that glows in the oceanic blue of the screen, drawn to it like a sun. A moth. And the pattern of its wings is a face, staring at me with lidless eyes. I wonder how it got in, which wormhole in the universe. This little cabin, I had thought, was secure. I have managed to keep out the light. But then: light has no mind of its own.

I think of killing it, but I don't. I didn't ask for company, but I can't help that it found me.

38.

When I returned from California, clouds of moths had come to live in our trees, their wings the colour of bone china. They came to kill, to ravage the birches and the oaks and the elms, to eat them alive from the outside in. It was strange to fear a thing as delicate as paper, something you could tear to shreds with your hands.

The moths fluttered low in the humid air outside the window as I unpacked. You bounced into my room. Let's play Winter, you said, dragging me by the hand, dragging me to the backyard. You pulled a half-smoked cigarette from your purse, lit it, and inhaled. You pretended that the smoke was your breath, frosting in cold air, and you made me try. We lazed beneath the trees while beads of sweat dripped down our necks and knotted our hair. We pretended to shiver, forcing our teeth to chatter. Our landlord painted the branches with Cygon. Fat larvae, the late bloomers, fell onto our skin as we sat in the grass while he worked.

Things are normal, right? you said.

I said: They never weren't normal though?

We didn't say anything more. We just sat there and watched the sentient tissue paper die and die and die.

39.

Baby–

This was a very hard email for me to write. I was very disappointed when we spoke on the phone last night. I was very excited to share my hopes and dreams for the future with the girl I love. I imagined, given that we are in a relationship, that you would be supportive of those hopes and dreams as a partner should be. Pursuing the career path of a foreign diplomat seems like a perfect trajectory for me. I already speak several languages and have lived in several different countries. I have been exposed to many different cultures and forms of government—let me tell you, things were very different in the Eastern Bloc.

It disappointed me greatly that when I shared my hopes and dreams with you, your initial reaction was concern that there are "no jobs available for a foreign diplomat's wife." Baby, this felt a little selfish to me. This isn't the 1950s. They don't expect a woman to just hop from country to country with her husband and not work. They make sure that the wife is able to work if she wants to—for instance, there is always secretarial work at the embassies. I know that secretarial work probably doesn't interest you, and I'm not saying you should do that as a career choice, but the option is there. Don't actors usually have day jobs anyway? Wouldn't being a secretary in an exotic country be more exciting than shining shoes or serving maraschino cherry-laced drinks to lecherous bankers? If you decide to continue acting, wouldn't it be a unique challenge to learn to act in other languages?

Baby, while your words hurt me, I'd like it if we could move on from this and have a fresh conversation about it when we are both feeling like our best (and most supportive) selves.

Sincerely,
D

40.

The actress returned. She was in your room, and it wasn't quiet. So I put on headphones and started educating myself about the Andes.

I pulled my laptop onto the bed and conjured a map: the mountain range spans the length of the continent, curving at Bolivia, curving like an old woman's spine. Millions of years ago, two tectonic plates collided and gave birth to mountains.

I wanted to share this with you, this marriage of poetry and geology. I wanted to tell you that extreme pressure and time can calcify to form a backbone.

This I would have liked to tell you less: there are several strings of mountains that meet occasionally in orographic knots, but often they don't meet at all, parallel lines that cannot touch.

I didn't want to share with you that South America is pushed westward at a rate of one and a half centimetres a year. I didn't want to tell you that the plates are never done moving, that they are the nomads of the planet's mantle.

It's not that I didn't like the information. It's just that I didn't know how to say it out loud without it sounding like a whole thing. It's just that saying it out loud would sound like lines from a play. It's just that they would sound like the lines that were the theme.

Sometimes there isn't any subtext. Sometimes you just want to talk about the Andes. Is it such a crime to talk about the Andes?

41.

Baby–

Yes, I was two years old when the Eastern Bloc dissolved. But I'll remind you that a way of life does not just evaporate with its government. It takes many years for things to change. My childhood, for all intents and purposes, was still one very much influenced by the Iron Curtain.

D.

42.

I can get you a job, said Anatole, but you won't like it. I made out with a guy in a bar once, and his dad runs a...*business*.

He took me to a butcher shop called The Big Butcher. The sign featured a cartoon man with very, very big biceps. A man looked up from flaking a ribeye when we entered. His biceps were average.

There was no interview. He asked me if I was a fainter, and I said no. I have fainted only once before, in kindergarten, on a class trip to the hospital. We were learning about what doctors do. In a multi-purpose room, we learned about stethoscopes, how to check for a heartbeat. A boy named Aaron put a stethoscope on my chest, and I watched his face listen for the rhythm.

It sounds weird, he said.

I have a heart murmur, I said. It's benign. Don't worry about it.

And then I hit the floor.

Yeah, I told the butcher, I don't faint.

The man took me to a back room and handed me a Spray-and-Vac. The floor was soaked with blood. Red blood, so fresh that the air hadn't blackened it yet.

The butcher pointed me toward three jugs of cleaning product. They were labelled with permanent marker on masking tape: DISINFECTANT, ORGANIC CLEANING SOLUTION, and ALKALINE. The butcher told me to ignore the labels because everything inside them was the same, and he left me to work.

It was soothing, cleaning the blood and remains. The Spray-and-Vac was powerful, and so was I. I was methodical; I went square by square, like Pac Man. I was very good. I was very talented at this line of work. I was better at this than I am at being an actor. I was better at this than I am at being an act-*ress*.

When I was finished, I could see the grout. It was as though no dead animals had ever entered that room. It was as though no dead things had ever entered that room or any other room either.

The butcher inspected my work. He gave me a parabola mouth of approval. Okay, he said, counting bills, you will come back tomorrow.

What will I do tomorrow? I said.

Little girl, he said, you will do the same thing all over again.

Sometimes, even now, I smell ammonia.

43.

When astronauts went to the moon, the dust clung to them, followed them back into the lander. There, where they could breathe again, where they could smell things, they noted that it smelled like old gunpowder. Like the wet ashes of a doused campfire.

The dust of Mars, I think, to people born there, will smell like red. The way that red candies taste red. They will wipe the dust from their boots and smell the red, rouge, scarlet, carmine, rose.

Except they won't know what a rose is.

44.

A heat wave and then another one and then another one. The world is a dumpster fire, said Anatole. He was lying like a starfish on the floor in a Speedo. He was once again crashing on our couch. You were using a plant mister to spray my face. We were taking turns. The actress wasn't there.

My phone tumbled to the floor and Anatole retrieved it with a clammy hand as it chimed. He stared at the phone screen. What does the D stand for, he asked.

Dick, you said.

I didn't correct you. I thought that maybe your voice had a certain kind of tone. It was a tone I liked.

45.

The heat turned into fever. First you, then me. Anatole sought refuge elsewhere. Everything was surrounded by light.

You texted me from the bath. *I forgot my tea on the counter*, it said. *Will you bring it to me?*

I fetched your tea. I knocked. Come in, you said in a hoarse but regal voice, as though you hadn't been expecting me.

The water was thick with bubbles and I felt relieved.

Do you want to get in? you said.

We had never taken a bath together. We had still barely even touched.

That's okay, I said. I'm too hot.

You coughed, your cheeks flushed. The heat of the bath and your hair and the fever made you uniformly red from the shoulder blades up. And still I could see you shivering.

I'm sorry I made you sick Velvet.

Can I stay? I said. I miss you when you're in the bath.

I miss *you* when I'm in the bath.

I curled into a fetal position on the bathmat and pressed my cheek against the side of the tub. It was surprisingly cool.

I think I'm dying, I said.

You aren't dying. *I'm* dying. Consumption.

If you died, I said, I would not survive it.

You took a deep breath. Tell me something I don't know about you, you said, in case this is our last conversation in the earthly realm.

I could hear the foam bubbles of the bath disintegrating. The air smelled medicinal, like eucalyptus. I felt delirious, uninhibited, like I might say anything. I opened my mouth to say one thing, but instead I said something else.

I have often longed for a country I have never seen, I said. It perforated my gap-toothed childhood with a dull pain, one that was akin to my belly protesting lactose or the naval lurch of roller coasters. Once I attempted to describe this to a school counsellor as an ache, and the things that made me ache included, but were not limited to: the smell of wet snow on pines; the last lines of television shows; a photograph of Prague's purpled cityscape at dusk, a two-page spread I tore from *National Geographic* and carried in my pencil case for years; Dickinson's "There's a Certain Slant of Light"; certain slants of light; any mention of the beaches of Normandy; the call of loons; the taste of clementines in December. The counsellor said I had an exaggerated case of ennui and wrote this in ballpoint pen and opened a fresh packet of folders to file away the assessment, and the smell of thick Manila paper gave me the funniest sensation in my gut.

We were both quiet for a long time. I coughed. Maybe I've had too much medication, I said.

Promise me we'll grow old together, you said. Okay? Promise me we'll always be friends.

I loved what you said.

I hated what you said.

46.

For as long as I can remember, I have concocted email passwords from the things of which I am most deeply ashamed. This way, I will never forget.

47.

You took a short contract north of the city. One month in a little tourist town, designing costumes for Shakespeare. Which Shakespeare? I said.

Who cares, you said.

On the day you left, I heard whale sounds I could not locate. I decided, since you had asked me to water your plants, that it would be permissible to see if these strange sounds were coming from your room.

I had never set foot in your room, and you had never set foot in mine. Once this had come up in conversation, and Anatole, who granted himself liberal entry to both our rooms, had been shocked. That's so weird! he said. You're so close! You're like, soulmates!

Now I crossed the threshold. The whales sang to one another, but in the distance, through walls. Your room was not the source, but still, I did not leave. I ran my hands tentatively along your velvet bedspread, the scraps of lace on your desk, buttons. Every surface was beautiful, like each was the subject of a still life painting. The candelabra on your dresser, a vase of dried lavender, a tiny brass bell. A mercury glass mirror on your nightstand, a piece of citrine.

Anatole, who was back, bustled around the corner. I jumped.
Oh, good, he said. I'm glad she tasked you with the watering.
I would kill everything.

He did not notice that I had no water. But he did notice a tube
on the floor, near the dresser.

Poor babe, he said, she forgot her fancy face cleanser.

I'd never seen the bottle in the shower or on the bathroom vanity.
I don't think she uses that, I said. Her skin is perfect, why would
she?

What are you talking about? said Anatole. Girl's gorgeous, but
she gets blemishes like everyone else.

I don't think I've ever seen a single blemish, I said. You were
always clean, always blemish free, always smooth.

You live with her though.

Yes, and her skin is always perfect.

You're so *nice*, said Anatole.

I suddenly remembered the last day of summer camp, when
everyone went around signing each other's T-shirts. I had been
too quiet for anyone to get to know me, and so everyone had
written, *you r so nice.*

I'm not nice, I said. I'm a fucking bitch.

Anatole laughed until he gave himself the hiccups.

She has the smoothest skin I've ever seen, I said.

Anatole stopped laughing slowly, wiping his eyes, staring at me.
We stood in your room for a long time, staring at each other.
Then he let out a long, low whistle.

Oh, babe, he said. You're in trouble.

48.

How's it going out there in the big wide world? I texted you.

Two days later, your name appeared on my phone. *I love it here.*
I think I'm going to change my name and run away to the country.

Can I come, I typed, but you did not answer.

We did not speak the rest of the time you were away.

49.

I decided to carve out my own interesting life in your absence. This was the belle époque, and baby—I was going to live.

I received a message from an old friend, a girl from my hometown. She was in the city, she said, to sort out a Visa extension before returning overseas. She was a perennial student heading off to a summer placement, a dig in Japan. She would be a doctor soon.

We met in a teashop and sat on the window ledge, on cushions. I tried to sit up straight. I had begun to wonder if I had bad posture.

At first the conversation was halting; we hadn't really kept in touch. I still have our letters, she said.

When we were in school we had called them notes, not letters. We had written each other at least one note every day for two years. Do you remember, she said, when I was sad, when my father left and I was diagnosed with endometriosis and I was in a very dark place? You wrote me the longest letter. It was a list, actually. One Hundred Reasons Why Life is Beautiful.

I don't remember that, I say. (I don't.) What was on the list?

Banana crepes, the Brontës, *The Legend of Zelda.*

What was one hundred?

Life is beautiful because someday it will be the future.

We drank our tea, sitting in the future.

My friend told me she was thinking of getting married. What's his name! I said.

It's a she, actually, said my friend.

I stammered an apology. I was shocked to have not known this about her. I wondered when she made the choice. Not choice. When she knew? I am a bigot, I thought. I must be a bigot.

My friend paid for my tea.

On the walk home, the evening air was sultry. I bought a doughnut and sat on a park bench, confectioner's sugar falling into the seams of my dress. I felt ill. Couples and groups sat on blankets on the grass with their covert bottles of wine and beer. A child tried to fly a kite. There was no wind. Children are idiots, I thought.

I tried to remember being a child.

I remembered one thing: an effeminate French boy named Henri-Claude, who had transferred halfway through the school year. He'd gotten into a fight with an older boy in the schoolyard because the older boy had declared that he was gay. The boy pushed Henri-Claude into a rose bush. A thorn pierced his nose.

It had been winter, and deep red blood stained the snow. The teachers had cleaned up Henri-Claude's nose, I remembered, but not the snow. It had stayed that way, a lurid memorial, until new snow covered it.

50.

I bought a hat that made me feel more like me than anything ever had before. It was second hand and cheap. I spent days plucking the previous owner's hairs from the brim. When you returned, you wouldn't even recognize me.

51.

Hi Baby—

Haven't heard from you in a little bit—I'm sure you must be busy. I know you hate FaceTime, but maybe it would be nice to see each other's faces. Ya know? Change things up. What do you think?

Love,
D

52.

The day before you returned, you posted a picture of me online. Missing this beauty, you captioned it.

53.

I decided to write you a letter. Times New Roman was more terrible than I remembered, so I decided to write the letter by hand. I made a pact with myself: if I finished, I meant every word.

54.

When you returned, I did not see you for several days; you were always gone when I woke, or missing when I went to sleep. The actress had a king-size bed, I'd heard you coyly say to Anatole once.

We made plans to go to dinner as though we didn't share a wall, as though we were two old friends who needed to catch up.

The restaurant I had chosen was too small. Our table was only an inch from the next table. It felt like the same table. The couple beside us were obviously on a first date.

I asked you about your time up north. It was a cute town, you said. Nice hat, you said.

The conversation tapered into nothing. I began to panic. I could tell you felt it too, playing with your coaster. What was happening? I longed for you to burst from my bedroom closet again.

Not wanting to give in to defeat, we found a noisy pub where talking didn't matter and fell into the safeness of a shared ritual: writing in our journals. That was a thing we liked to do together: sit side by side, documenting our days for posterity. And whoever died first would have the responsibility of burning the other's journals or bestowing them to an important museum collection should we become prolific.

Sitting across the table felt too far from you. I wanted something, something, something else. I wanted to stop feeling like I was swimming in your aura. I wanted a lobotomy. I wanted everything to be normal.

We started chatting with a group of boys from Scotland. They joined our table and it soon became cluttered with empty pint glasses and rings of condensation.

And then I noticed that my journal was missing. You understood the severity of this situation, a lost journal. You helped me look through my backpack four, five times; under the table; under coats. You made the Scottish boys look.

I went to the bartender. It's a red book, I said. It's a very important book.

She shook her head.

The escalation of my panic began to confuse you. At least it was a new journal, you said. You'd just started it a couple of weeks ago, right?

It's very private, I said. No one can read it. Someone is going to find it and read it!

Everything I had ever felt was visible on my face. You studied my face, curious.

I went to the bathroom and cried, trying not to cry, drunk and trying not to be drunk. I held toilet paper under my eyes to catch the tears as they fell.

A girl with a very blonde perm walked into the bathroom. Oh baby girl, she said, he is not worth it. And then she put her arms around me. She held me like this. We swayed a little. She tried to kiss my cheek, I think, but we were swaying, and she kissed the corner of my mouth.

I hate him for hurting you, she slurred.

I returned to the bartender once more, remembering. It was in a paper bag! I said, frenzied. I slipped it into a bag of leftovers from a restaurant. I can tell you exactly what was inside.

And then, with relief, I saw the corner of that bag poking out between the beer fridge and the cash register.

On the walk home, you were quiet. You can tell me anything, you know, you said finally.

Thanks, I said.

That night, after I heard you leave the apartment, I opened my journal. On the first page I had written your name three times, and then: *when will that no longer be the case?*

It was the only page on which your name appeared.

55.

Baby–

You said in your last email that you have been living on a diet of "bread and canned beans." Was this a joke? Have you ever thought about getting your blood sugar levels checked? North American breads contain an obscene amount of sugars. Have you ever noticed that hot dog buns taste like cake? Honestly, the bun is almost as bad for you as the wiener. Maybe you ought to think about having some blood tests done? Also, did you know that aside from bread containing sugar (which is an opiate, by the way) it also contains sawdust? Look it up.

Kindly,
D

56.

I searched, *how to have a female friend*. The WikiHow tutorial
had many colourful illustrations.

Part One: Making Her Acquaintance.

Step One: Take any opportunity to meet potential friends.
Step Two: Start a Conversation.
Step Three: Present your best self.
Step four: Practice friendliness.

How does a person practice friendliness? I said to nobody. The
cartoons all depicted men learning to be friends with women.

Part Two: Getting to know each other.

Step One: Discuss your interests.
Step Two: Listen intently.
Step Three: Maintain your independence and insert your opinions.

Insert, like the sharp tips of cloves into an orange rind? Like a
penis into a vagina?

Step Four: Enjoy mutual new activities.
Step Five: Make compromises.
Step Six: Stay positive and fun.

Part Three: Deepening your friendship.

Step One: Share your feelings.
Step Two: Incorporate her into your circle.
Step Three: Follow up with her.
Step Four: Enjoy more time together.

The last step was accompanied by an illustration of a man and a woman jogging in gym shorts together, an orange sunset behind them.

57.

Come with me to the hospital, I said to Anatole. You'll love it. We can steal a baby.

We'll have to clean up if we steal a baby, Anatole said, pointing. There are scissors on the floor and that's just where they go.

I was dizzy from the fasting, which was for the blood tests. Anatole was dizzy because he was fasting in solidarity—he said it made drugs work faster.

What would we name our stolen baby? I mused. He sat on the bed and watched while I pulled a sundress over my head.

Something unusual, he said. Something everyone's forgotten. Our parents' generation destroyed names. We have nicknames and surnames and place names and words that aren't words for names. We'll name our baby something classic. Winston. Elizabeth. Gertrude.

No one will know how to spell it, I said, swaying.

Is our baby stupid? he said.

I feel strange, I said, running my hands through my hair. I thought it was the hunger. I want meat. But it's more than that. It's the bright edge of everything. Even you.

Did you know you're a brunette? Jesus, you've got hair for days. I love it, he said, petting it. It's nicer than your curtains. Except at the ends. It's dead at the ends. I could cut it for you—the scissors.

No, I said, never, because then how would I do this?

And I got up on the bed and tucked my head between my knees. The hair spilled over me, obscuring everything. I'm invisible, I said, try and find me.

58.

Why are hospitals quiet? I said. Why do they echo? Why do they smell like chemicals, like factory, cleaner, new car, condoms?

Shh, Anatole said, try to whisper.

We followed yellow dots on the floor toward a waiting area with plastic chairs and C-SPAN playing in the corner. A plane had crashed in water, there were sad people on TV, a vigil, candles in cups. The waiting room was half-full, people with rings beneath their eyes, people with coughs, people who looked perfectly fine on the outside. There was one woman, maybe she was fifty. Her feet did not touch the floor. She wore a paper mask over her mouth. No one sat beside this woman. She lifted her eyes from the floor and looked right at me. Then she looked away, folded her hands in her lap. I had the feeling that if I didn't sit beside her, I would break her heart. So I took a number and sat beside the woman, who looked sideways at me as I did so. Her hands looked soft and shiny, the way skin looks after it's been freshly waxed. Or burned.

I was not afraid of my neighbour. Maybe I was the danger. Maybe she was afraid of me, afraid of the air I carried. I started to take shallow breaths so that she would not feel threatened.

Why do you look like you're going to faint? said Anatole, plunking himself in the seat beside me.

I don't faint, I said.

He looked at the number in my hand: sixty-eight. *So close*, he said, stroking the little tag.

I counted heads in the room. I counted three times, because that's how long it took to get it right. There were sixteen people in the room. The number on the Now Serving sign was forty-five. Twenty-three people ahead of us. How does that happen? How do hospitals work? Was there a VIP room for the missing? Was my math the proper math?

I glanced discreetly at my neighbour's soft hands. I could see that her tag said seventy. Wasn't she here when we arrived?

Anatole stared at the ground. Every now and then, he'd nudge me, bring his finger right down to the floor. Do you see it, he would say, tracing the flecks in the tile. What does that look like to you?

The Creation of Adam, I said. Rutabaga. The gap between Elton John's teeth.

He kept studying the floor like a serious academic. It's such a beautiful floor, he said. Maybe I'll ask them what it is. I'd like to have it in my own house someday.

Sixty-eight, flickered the sign. So close.

59.

Six vials? I said.

Yes, six, said the nurse, laying six vials on a little plastic table. Half a baker's dozen, he said.

I said: A baker's dozen is thirteen. I would feel more comfortable with a number that is closer to one.

He said: That wouldn't be enough blood for all the tests.

I said: I think you'll find my blood to be voracious.

Make a fist.

I don't want to.

Come on now.

I said: I'm only here to see about the sawdust. Is there another way for you to check that? Is there another way for you to check that though?

But the needle was in my arm, and I didn't like that. I didn't like that at all. And it's my arm and I am the governor of my arm and I didn't like what was happening, so I started to untie the rubber band around it.

Not yet, said the nurse, I need you to relax.

And I said: You know what, I think just stop it right now.

But the blood was coming so he couldn't stop it because gravity wasn't working. So I just kept giving orders that weren't followed while he collected half a baker's dozen of something that wasn't red at all. It was just India ink. If it left my body I couldn't keep it red.

I said: I don't want to do this anymore.

I picked up my phone and the nurse said: Sorry, no phones.

But I dialed anyway. I could hear it ringing in the southern climate, sound waves shimmering in the heat. The line clicked.

I don't want to be together anymore, I said.

My boyfriend said: You're dizzy because of the blood tests.

I said nothing.

My boyfriend said: Can you hear me?

I said nothing.

My boyfriend said: Did you eat a cookie?

I hung up.

You see, I said to the nurse, as he removed the rubber band, I am wholly untethered.

60.

We ate in the hospital cafeteria, which Anatole said was the saddest restaurant he'd ever seen. We ate sandwiches at plastic tables. Our hot skin stuck to the chairs. Anatole ate all of his in one bite. He leaned back and patted his stomach. Then he reached into his bag, held an empty soda cup beneath the table, mixed an afternoon cocktail. He seemed frantic, desperate to get the straw in his mouth.

I looked around the cafeteria. We didn't have a cafeteria in my school, I said.

No?

Well we did, but then we had to eat in our classrooms because budget cuts meant they had to annex the cafeteria for more classrooms, I said.

Did you go to a sad school for poor little orphans during the Industrial Revolution? said Anatole.

I pushed the rest of my sandwich toward Anatole because I wasn't hungry. I watched him eat and remembered how we would collect our lunch trays from the canteen or pull our lunch bags from our cubicles and eat at our desks. Unsupervised.

The children in my class developed a game, I said. The Next Person Who Walks Through the Door Is Gay.

The fuck?

I hated ordering from the canteen because I hated having to return to the classroom and become Gay, I said.

I remembered the walk from the door, eyes and snickers following me to my desk. I would feel relieved when another child entered the room to taunts and became More Gay than me.

Children are so fucking mean, said Anatole. He wolfed down the last of my sandwich. You should've eaten that, he said.

I feel like dancing, I said in a fever. Do you feel like dancing?

My phone lit up with a text from you: *Aquarium?*

We can dance there, he said.

61.

There was a line for the aquarium that snaked around the corner, sweaty children, sweaty parents, teenagers in clothing that hung loosely, revealing bathing suits underneath. You found us in the line and hugged us both, even though we'd seen each other only hours earlier, before you'd left for your brunch shift. There was no sign of the actress. There are sharks, you promised, that swim above your head.

Inside, there were fish that sucked the glass too. Fish the size of me and things that slithered. Fish that looked like plants, appendages like seaweed or coral. Where does the thinking go, I wondered. Where does the hunger form, the instincts happen? Do they start in a branch of what might be the spine? Do they recognize their own young?

By the ticket kiosk there was an indoor lake that smelled like a pool. But I thought the smell of a pool was chlorine, and wouldn't chlorine kill fish? That was confusing. I felt extremely confused.

This pool was surrounded by a low railing, bars that reached my abdomen, and all around the lake there was plant life, things meant to thrive in damp places. This is where they keep the sharks, you said.

I leaned over the railing. Shouldn't the railing be higher, then? I said. It looked remarkably low to me and I was hot and the water looked inviting. Couldn't, I said, couldn't a child just jump right over? Well, couldn't they? There isn't even a warning sign.

Maybe they aren't the kind of sharks that eat children, Anatole offered.

The rail was getting slippery beneath my hands. Also, I said, how do we get to see them? Do we have to wait until something draws them to the surface, like a diving child?

You looked at Anatole. He shrugged. Everything ok? you said.

Oh yes, I said, I am wholly untethered.

62.

We found jellyfish. Little ones, the size of buttons, milky as full moons. They moved with seeming determination, their entire bodies convulsing in an effort to propel themselves through lit tanks. Children tapped the glass, mimicked the motion with their mouths. But the crowd seemed to be concentrated further up the hall, the observers in rows six or seven people thick in front of the glass. What's all this? said Anatole. I need to go to there.

We pushed our way through the crowd, all those bodies anchored like rocks to split a stream. And the moment we saw them, the thing everyone was looking at, we were breathless.

Bioluminescent life. Jellyfish, the size of our heads, pulsating in a tank that spanned floor to ceiling. They glowed, either by some extraordinary display of nature or an effective illusion— I couldn't tell which. Their long tendrils dilated and curled like hair.

The mass of people standing before the glass was almost impossible to penetrate. We wove through the tightly packed bodies. Anatole was sucked into the crowd, away from us. We were trapped in some kind of man sandwich, you and I. Men with baseball hats, men with kids, men in Hawaiian shirts, bald men, mannish-looking men. These are some of the oldest creatures on Earth, you whispered, and I giggled because I didn't know if you were talking about the jellyfish or the men.

Your body was pressed against mine, our tattoos touching. Your eyes flickered between the tank and a series of information placards on the wall beside it. Some jellyfish have light-sensitive organs, you said, and this is how they determine up from down, because the sunlight comes from above. A group of jellyfish is called a bloom, you said, or also a smack, and they have lived on Earth for millions of years. They have no brains. They can detect pain, but not feel it; they can respond to pain by moving faster, changing direction, but they can never understand or process it.

And then we were both silent for a long time. I think I might be a jellyfish, you said at last. I could very well be a jellyfish.

And then I felt it: your hand sliding up the hem of my skirt, the crowd affording us privacy. Your fingers tugging my underwear, lingering there. You fingers inside me, twirling themselves in all that new silk. And I knew.

And so I reached for you too. As if to say: I understand. As if to say: We're the same. As if to say: Who needs the trappings of language when you can say it with the tips of your fingers.

The crowd jostled us from behind and your fingers shot away. You looked at me, your face glowing red in the light of the ancient life.

I've been thinking about it, I said quietly, and I love you.

What? you said.

I said: Should I die, drown, and decay, only to return one day in some other form, I would hope only to share with you one primordial piece of time and space. I would desire no fanfare but a simple place for you and I alone. If our second life could be spent as two hinges in the jawbone of a lesser fish, scale-linked in some green and dark deep, I would think as we learn to newly forgo chewing, to be wet: love is enough.

What? you said.

I just needed a sign from you, I said, a sign. I was so afraid. But a sign was all I needed.

You blinked like a guillotine. What sign?

That thing you did just now.

I didn't do anything at all, you said.

The way you touched—

And we both looked down at your hands. We both looked down at your hands deep inside your pockets.

63.

Here is what I have learned about fainting: your head can't be any higher than your heart. If you just lie down, maybe you won't faint. If I had lain down on the cold tile floor, maybe I wouldn't have fainted. Maybe if I hadn't started to walk away from you the minute you started screaming *assault*, screaming for security, maybe I wouldn't have fainted. Maybe if I had just stopped to take a nap as you told the man sandwich to *back the fuck up*, maybe I wouldn't have fainted.

Maybe if I hadn't heard you demand which of those bastards had laid a hand on your friend, maybe I wouldn't have fainted. Maybe if the word *friend* hadn't echoed down the sound chamber of my ear and all the people in the jellyfish room and all the jellyfish hadn't turned to watch, maybe then I wouldn't have fainted.

What I have also learned about fainting is: you can't just faint when you need to. You can't just faint when you would like everything to stop. If I had stayed where I was, maybe I would have fainted properly. Maybe if I hadn't started to walk away and then started to run, maybe I wouldn't have tripped and hit the iron railing with the side of my face.

64.

Astronauts struggle to cry in space because tears don't fall—they gather and cling to the eyeball in one globular bead. Astronauts learn not to cry because space tears sting.

65.

The doctor said: Don't panic. He said: You won't be able to open your mouth for many weeks, but you didn't even crack a tooth, you lucky girl.

I wanted to say: The most comfortable feeling in the world is the moment after anesthesia and the moment before the memory and the pain, and can I have that again, is there a way?

66.

Astronauts launched two thousand four hundred and seventy-eight jelly polyps and babies into space aboard the *Columbia* shuttle to monitor the effects of weightlessness on juvenile organisms. When the babies returned to Earth, they could not tell up from down.

67.

The police came and I could not speak, so they left.

68.

I thought about food. I thought about foods I hated. I thought about button cap mushrooms. I thought about Bounty bars. I thought about liver and creamed corn. I thought a lot about liver, which never stops looking like an organ, no matter how you cook it or disguise it. You could julienne liver and it would still look like the remains of a living thing, an organ strained through a barbed wire fence. I wanted it.

69.

I started to think in the imaginative conditional. If I were to speak, I would—

I remembered things I read somewhere once and had promptly forgotten. Female birds only have one ovary. If they had two ovaries, they would be too heavy to fly. Michelangelo hated painting. The Saxon word for the first month of the year was *Wulfmonath*, the month when starving wolves were bold enough to enter the villages.

70.

Anatole brought me magazines and left them on the night table. He said that the magazines were from both of you but that you had to work and you were sorry you couldn't come but hoped I was okay.

After he left, I did not read them. Instead, I watched television and pretended that I was in a hotel. I watched heterosexual couples argue about houses overseas that they may or may not buy and then buy and then change. I watched cartoons. I watched the news and wondered why anchors never wear patterned clothing. I thought that we are probably a distractible species.

Have you ever dreamed, said an anchor in a bright blue pattern-less dress, about visiting a distant planet?

Did you pee in the bedpan? said a nurse.

Have you ever fantasized about being the first person to set foot on Mars? said the anchor.

Did you? Because I should empty it if you did.

Well, here's your opportunity. A not-for-profit organization has claimed to be the first with a feasible plan for reaching the Red Planet!

Earth to the Terminator, said the nurse. The nurses had taken to calling me the Terminator because I had metal plates in my jaw now. The first time a nurse called me the Terminator, I opened my mouth to respond but couldn't. I just grimaced. They mistook my grimace for a smile and continued to call me the Terminator, hoping to bait more smiles.

Sound exciting? Well, said the anchor, there's a catch. The lucky few will be chosen based on a rigorous application and screening process, but before you start putting yours together, there's something they want you to know.

Did you do a number two in the bedpan?

The journey to Mars is a one-way ticket. If you go...you go forever. Interested? For details on the application process, the organization invites you to visit their website at...

I wanted to text you that the Mars thing was on TV because we didn't own a TV and you were missing it. I wondered if the actress had a TV. I wanted to tell you that I'd thought of one more thing that takes one minute to accomplish. In one minute, a person could:

Microwave a small portion of leftovers
Find the correct key on a keychain of many identical keys
Trim the stems of one dozen roses
Walk down seven flights of stairs
Die from a brain aneurysm
Make an application video for Mars

In one minute, a person could also:

End a friendship with a woman

Earth to the Terminator, said the nurse.

Stay tuned for the weather, said the anchor. We'll be back right after this.

71.

I would like to report a sexual assault. I held up my phone screen, where the words were written.

We know, they said. Your friends—it's been reported. That's why we're here.

They're nice, I thought. The police were talking to me like I was a little girl, and I didn't even get mad. I just thought: How nice. I thought: They're being nice because they don't know the full story yet.

We've got our people looking at the security camera footage, they said.

My phone battery died, so I signaled for one of the officers to give me a pen and paper. She looked at my night table, which contained only a stale cup of juice and many magazines, and the night table of the patient beside me, which contained only flowers and a Polly Pocket. Then the officer handed me her official police pad, and I wished she would leave the room so I could look at her notes on other cases, other bad people.

I wrote: *A different assault. One I did.*

What?

I accidentally assaulted my friend when I was assaulted because I didn't know it wasn't her and I thought I was reciprocating something. So I did a bad thing.

The police read my pad, looked at each other. How much morphine is she on? I heard one of them mutter to a nurse with an armful of binders.

Oh, an elephant's load, said the nurse.

When will I have to go to jail, I wrote.

Later, when the officers were gone, I wrote a note to my neighbour asking if I could play with her Polly Pocket. She told me that I had to wash my hands first. I washed my hands, and then I made the little plastic family sit down and have a nice meal together.

72.

I awoke in the middle of the night, badly needing to pee. The nurses wanted me to use the bedpan, but I shook my head, struggling to be understood through my clamped jaw. I felt physically capable of going to the bathroom. The thing that I clung to during my hospital stay was manners. I wanted to be a good person. I bookended my requests of the nurses with *please* and *thank you*. Now I said: I would like to use the toilet, thank you. The words were as clear as heavy cotton, but I made them understand.

They deliberated. The problem, I realized, was that they did not want me to look in the mirror. You'll panic, they said.

I saw them see me, wondering what it was they saw, what my face had become. I wondered, even in my drugged state, whether they were worried because I was a girl. Did they fear the depths of my vanity, the extent to which it could be bruised?

They agreed to let me go to the washroom with the lights off. They helped me from the bed, but when one nurse tried to shut the door it became clear that I would be navigating in complete darkness. Someone relented and turned on a light. It was all very confusing.

I peed and stood to wash my hands. And then I looked at myself in the mirror.

I saw the grotesque souvenirs of my body's reaction to surgery. My usual under-eye circles were now as plush as the pillows of a ring box, my eyes like grommets in an overstuffed sofa, straining to contain the fabric. And my mouth. No longer a mouth, or existing where a mouth exists: instead, a violent and enormous gash, spreading to all the regions of my bruised face. It was twisted, the lips puffed and angry. One corner stretched somewhere near my cheekbone, the other towards my ear. My lips were trapped in a grin.

High as a dirigible, I turned my face to the side as much as I could without having to slide my eyes from my reflection. I placed the tip of one finger beneath my nose and let the knucklebone rest against my chin, the international signal for *shh*.

My twisted, bruised face was the most beautiful thing I had ever seen because it matched my insides. I had never felt such elation looking in a mirror. I smiled at myself, warm with morphine. The corners of my mouth twitched.

And then I threw up. It was like a horror film, black blood and bile dripping from the wires of my clamped teeth. Nurses came into the room, reassuring me that this was normal, that my body was trying to rid itself of all the blood that had dripped down my throat during surgery. I was scolded for looking in the mirror. It's temporary, one nurse said kindly. All of this is temporary.

I love my face, I slurred. Or tried to, but the wires and the blood and the swelling turned my words into the whine of an injured animal. They tried to escort me back to bed. I was happy; couldn't they see that? I had never been so happy. I'm *smiling*, I howled incomprehensibly to an unseen moon.

73.

A man put his hands in my mouth and that was okay because he was a doctor and he was doing a proper doctor thing. He was taking out the wires. Still no solid foods for at least a month, he said. Chewing and speaking now will be like trying to run a marathon after wearing a cast for a very long time.

74.

When I came home from the hospital, I was not allowed to pick anything up because I was not allowed to burn extra calories because I could eat only blended-up noodle soup and air. But alone in my room, I took a special pleasure in picking things up and putting them down again. A hairbrush. A book. A mini succulent. I noticed something shiny between the old floorboards and pried it out with my fingernail. The metal back of an earring. I blew away the dust bunny and the strands of hair and rolled it around in the palm of my hand, like I was Hercules.

75.

You knocked on my door. Can we talk? you said.

I let you remember that I could not. I let the silence do the talking for me. When I heard your footsteps disappearing down the hall, I pulled out a *National Geographic* with Mars on the cover. I scoured the Internet for a cheap video camera. I browsed Airbnb. I lifted a bunch of things and laid them down again, but instead of laying them down where they belonged, I laid them in a suitcase.

I packed the letter I kept writing to you and never delivered. The last thing I had written was:

Do you know how they make orange juice? The factory kind? Oranges are carted from the grove and here the good old days end: they are squeezed of their juice, which is placed in giant vats for processing— that is, the stripping of oxygen, to keep it from spoiling for one year. But this also strips the juice of its flavor, and so the flavor has to be added to it artificially. Sometimes I think of tears this way. When they meet oxygen, the truth must be returned.

76.

The vocal cords do not atrophy. I press record and open my mouth, just a little, and the hinges scream in protest and I see stars, a whole galaxy clapping its hand over my mouth. My throat is a vacuum for the last sounds in the world.

I turn off the camera and take out the memory card. I open my jaw just a tiny little bit, and I've forgotten what solids are like, so I bite the memory card. I wish I could eat this.

There is a knock that isn't a sound I've made. It's the door. There's a knock on the door and when I answer, it's

—you.

It's you, standing there framed against the sun and sea with a little suitcase on wheels.

Anatole says you want to go to Mars, you say.

I fetch a pen and paper. Yes, I scribble. I'm here to work on my application video. I point to the camera.

You know that call for submissions was a hoax, right?

No. It was very detailed. There's a whole process.

How can they send you to Mars if they can't figure out how to send you that close to the sun without the radiation killing you?

What?

MIT released a report. We can't colonize Mars for another thirty years at least.

I sit down on the bed. You don't close the door. The sun is very bright. I'd forgotten about the sun. I'd also forgotten about the moth, but it has not forgotten the sun. It flies through the open door like it's being summoned. I stare at the light on the water like it's porn. I stare at it like I could really get off on it. I think: I could do without it though. I think: I don't need it. I think: Light is a privilege, and all of mine should be revoked.

You move to take my hand, but I pull it away because my hand shouldn't get to touch you like that. I pick up the pen and hold that instead. I hold that, and I make the pen say: I did a bad thing and I'm sorry.

You didn't do a bad thing, you say. A bad thing happened to you.

You lift a hand like it's maybe to cover my mouth, to silence me. But you lift the other hand too and place one on either side of my face, over my swollen jaw. Anatole said the doctor said you'd be able to speak by now, you say. But it's okay if you're not ready to speak yet.

You open your suitcase. You take out a loaf of bread. He also said you'd be able to eat solids by now, you say. You place a slice of bread on the plate and cut it into tiny squares. It's the body of Christ, you say. If you don't eat it, he'll feel insecure.

You slide the plate in front of me and spear a piece of bread on a fork. Only if you're ready, you say.

Ready for what? I say—but I don't say, because I can't yet.

And anyway, you already know what I'm saying.

ACKNOWLEDGEMENTS

While *Jawbone* was originally written as a short novel, it had a brief life as a stage adaptation. With theatre comes community, and I am tremendously grateful for the community that has supported this book along the way, in every iteration.

Thank you to Nightwood Theatre's Write from the Hip program: Andrea Donaldson, Kelly Thornton, and my cohort of fellow playwrights: Andrea Scott, Nick Green, Monica Garrido, Chelsea Woolley, Intisar Awisse, and Ali Joy Richardson. Thank you to Hannah Moscovitch for the dramaturgical wisdom.

Thanks to Brittany Pack, Meagan Braem, Christine Brubaker, and the University of Calgary for the workshop production.

Thanks to Ruth Lawrence of White Rooster Theatre for producing the world premiere. Thanks to Mallory Clarke for holding my hand through the loneliness of space (i.e. a solo performance), and thank you to Brooke Adams, Ryan Wilcox, Bob Stamp, Brian Kenny, and Alison Helmer for creating a world around me.

Thanks to Paul Carlucci for the careful editorial insight, and to Debra Bell and the entire team at Radiant for believing in the power of shorter works.

Thanks to Terry Doyle for being a most discerning reader.

Thanks to Lisa Moore, Robert Finley, Nancy Pedri, and Memorial University of Newfoundland's English Department for granting me the time, space, and financial support as Writer in Residence to finish revisions for this book.

Thanks to my family: Wenda, Neville, Mitchell, Ryan, Meaghan, and Maddie, for tethering me to earth.

Thanks to Stephen Dunn, Erin Eaton, James Hawksley, Jamie Mac, James March, Santiago Guzmán, Mihalis Barry, Allison Kelly, Charlie Tomlinson, Aron Rosenberg, Amelia Manuel, and all of the Anatoles.

MEGHAN GREELEY is a writer, performer, and director. Her prose, poetry, and scripts have been published in *The Stockholm Review of Literature*, *Ephemera*, Metatron's ÖMËGÄ project, *Riddle Fence*, *Humber Mouths 2*, *The Breakwater Book of Contemporary Newfoundland Plays (Vol. 1)*, and the Playwrights Canada Press anthology *Long Story Short*. Her stage play *Hunger*, published by Breakwater Books, was a finalist for the 2023 Winterset Award. She was a 2016 nominee for the RBC Tarragon Emerging Playwrights Prize and was later a resident of both the Tarragon Playwrights Unit and Nightwood Theatre's Write from the Hip program. Her stage plays have been performed in Toronto, Halifax, Calgary, and across Newfoundland. She was the 2023 Writer-in-Residence at Memorial University's Department of English, and is currently the Artistic Director of White Rooster Theatre and the Creative Nonfiction Editor at *Riddle Fence*. Meghan lives in St. John's, Newfoundland.